P9-DWW-346

Zach AND Lucy
and the
Yoga Zoo

By the Pifferson Sisters
Illustrated by Mark Chambers

Ready-to-Read

Simon Spotlight
New York   London   Toronto   Sydney   New Delhi

SIMON SPOTLIGHT
An imprint of Simon & Schuster Children's Publishing Division
1230 Avenue of the Americas, New York, New York 10020
This Simon Spotlight edition February 2016
Text copyright © 2016 by Jennifer Bradbury and Stephanie Guerra
Illustrations copyright © 2016 by Mark Chambers
For information about special discounts for bulk purchases, please contact Simon & Schuster
Special Sales at 1-866-506-1949 or business@simonandschuster.com.
Manufactured in the United States of America 0116 LAK
2 4 6 8 10 9 7 5 3 1
Library of Congress Cataloging-in-Publication Data
Pifferson Sisters. Zach and Lucy and the yoga zoo / by the Pifferson Sisters ;
illustrated by Mark Chambers. pages cm. — (Ready-to-read) Summary: Lucy and Zach set up
a yoga studio in the basement of their apartment building using potted plants from the lobby,
doormats taken from various neighbors, and their very limited knowledge of yoga,
on a day when snooty Mrs. Blankenship is giving her book club a tour.
ISBN 978-1-4814-3938-1 (trade pbk. : alk. paper) —
ISBN 978-1-4814-3939-8 (hardcover : alk. paper) — ISBN 978-1-4814-3940-4 (eBook)
[1. Yoga—Fiction. 2. Brothers and sisters—Fiction. 3. Apartment houses—Fiction.
4. Behavior—Fiction. 5. Humorous stories.]
I. Chambers, Mark, 1980- illustrator. II. Title.
PZ7.1.P54Zam 2016
[Fic]—dc23
2014049370

CONTENTS

CHAPTER 1:
Upside Down

Lucy and Zach live in apartment 2B in the Royal Amherst Building.

Lucy is the older sister, and she likes to make things up.

Zach is the younger brother, and he likes to make things happen.

They stay out of trouble—most of the time.

The Royal Amherst Building is a tall, old brick building with long hallways, an elevator with lots of buttons, and a doorman named Ned. It's in a big city, on a busy street full of stores, people, and parks.

Lucy and Zach can go almost anywhere on the block, as long as they stay together.

Lucy and Zach think their neighborhood is perfect for all sorts of things.

Some think it was perfect before Lucy and Zach got there.

One rainy morning, Lucy and Zach went to the living room to build a pillow fort—and they found their mom standing on her head!

"What are you *doing*?" asked Zach.

"Yoga," said their mom.

"Can we do it too?" asked Lucy.

"No, I need quiet," said their mom.

"Lucy, headstands are for experts only."

Suddenly, a soothing voice from the TV said, "Pigeon"—and their mom did the splits!

Zach and Lucy watched in amazement as the TV lady said, "Crab! Plank! Tree!" and their mom twisted into funny shapes.

"Who is she?" Zach asked.

"She's a yoga teacher," explained their mom. "It costs a lot of money to take her classes, but I can do them for free at home."

Lucy whispered to Zach, "What if *we* teach yoga?"

He gave her a strange look. "But we don't know how to do yoga."

"It looks easy. Plus, we could charge kids in the building a lot of money to come!"

"I don't know," said Zach.

"Trust me," said Lucy.

CHAPTER 2:
Mostly Quiet

"We're going to have a yoga class," Lucy announced. "Okay, Mom?"

Their mom was trying to touch her toes for something the TV lady called Happy Baby. "Fine," she said. "Just remember the rules—"

"Stay together, stay on the block, and don't bother Mrs. Blankenship!" Lucy called as they rushed out into the hall.

Zach and Lucy needed the perfect place to set up their yoga class. It had to be big. It had to be close. And it had to be out of the way of certain neighbors.

"Why do you need the basement today?" Ned asked. He was in charge of the door, the keys, the basement, and lots of other important things.

"We're going to do a yoga class," Lucy explained.

"Hmm," Ned began. "Yoga is quiet, right?"

"Sure," said Lucy.

"Mostly," added Zach.

"Okay, good," said Ned. "Because Mrs. Blankenship's book club is coming over today, and I'd like to make sure they don't hear anything upstairs." He flipped on the lights. "Understand?"

"Yes!" Lucy said.

Zach and Lucy got the room ready.

"Will our friends really pay for this?"
Zach asked, looking around. "It doesn't
look right."

"Let's go back upstairs and see what the
TV lady has in *her* class," said Lucy.

Zach and Lucy peeked into the living room and watched their mom's video for a moment.

"There are lots of plants," whispered Lucy.

"And everybody has towels," said Zach.

"And mats," said Lucy.

"And there's funny music playing," said Zach.

Zach and Lucy each grabbed a garbage bag and began to fill it with supplies.

"Now what?" Zach asked.

"Now we find customers," said Lucy.

CHAPTER 3:
A Close Call

Zach and Lucy went to see all their friends in the Royal Amherst Building. Their first stop was at Oliver's apartment.

"We're having a yoga class," said Lucy. "It costs twenty-five cents. Do you want to come?"

"What's yoga?" asked Oliver.

"A game where you do the splits and other fun things," said Lucy.

"You can pretend to be different animals," added Zach.

"Okay!" said Oliver. "Let me tell my mom."

"Wear something comfortable," Lucy told him. "We'll wait for you."

Oliver came back in a moment, wearing his pajamas.

Lisa in 3F said she wanted to do yoga too. She changed into her pajamas and joined them.

"Can I wear my superhero outfit?" Henry in 4H asked when they invited him. Zach and Lucy said that was fine.

Sydney in 5A decided to wear her bathing suit. She didn't have twenty-five cents, so she paid with stickers instead.

Zach and Lucy were leading their customers to the elevator when they heard a loud noise down the hall. It was ladies. Lots of them.

"The Royal Amherst was built one hundred years ago," someone said in a loud voice. "It has always been a very elegant place to live."

Zach and Lucy looked at each other. They knew that voice.

"Quick!" Zach said. "Get in the elevator before Mrs. Blankenship sees us!"

CHAPTER 4:
One More Thing

The basement looked great. And it looked even more like the video now that it was filled with friends ready to do yoga.

"Wait!" Lucy stared at the floor. "We forgot the mats!"

"Who's Matt?" Henry asked. "And when do we do yoga? I have to be home by—"

"Everybody needs to get one more thing before we can start," Zach said. "Follow me."

Zach thought the mat he found would be just the thing for their yoga class.

Sydney picked one that had lots of pretty flowers on it.

And Henry and Oliver had another near miss with Mrs. Blankenship's book club.

CHAPTER 5:
Wild Animals

Finally, they were ready to begin. "Now can we do yoga?" Sydney whined.

"Yes!" Lucy said. "Stand on your mat and get ready."

All the kids stood on their mats. They looked at Lucy.

Lucy looked back at them.

Someone coughed.

Someone else sighed.

"So?" Sydney asked. "Aren't you going to start?"

Lucy frowned. "Ummm . . . ," she said. "Well . . ."

"You don't even know how to do yoga!" said Henry.

Lucy turned red.

"Yes, we do!" Zach said. "First, you pretend to be a dog." He dropped down on his hands and knees.

Sydney watched for a moment. Then she crouched, stuck out her tongue, and barked. "Woof!"

"Grrrr," said Henry, and he showed his teeth.

The kids were different kinds of dogs. Sydney was a small, yippy dog. Henry was a big, slobbery dog. Oliver and Lisa were loud, fast dogs.

"Now, go like this," said Zach. He stood up, stretched his arms out, and said in a slow, calm voice, "Take a deep breath."

But the dogs were barking too loudly to hear him.

Before they could get too out of hand, Zach tried something else. "Pigeon!"

Everybody flapped their wings and strutted.

"Bawk bawk!" said Henry. And he pecked Sydney on the head!

"Hey!" she said. Then she roared, "I'm a cheetah, and I eat pigeons!" She began to chase Henry.

"I'm a crab!" yelled Oliver.

"I'm a hummingbird!" said Lisa, flapping her arms.

"You're doing it wrong!" said Zach.
But nobody listened.
Not even Lucy. "I'm a T. rex!" she said
and kicked over a plant.

CHAPTER 6:
A Mix-Up

They were having so much fun, and they were making so much noise, that none of them heard the footsteps outside the door—or the voice in the hallway.

"This served as our common room when I was a young lady," Mrs. Blankenship said as she opened the door. "I once took tea with the cousin of the Duke of—"

"Irene?" one of the old ladies asked Mrs. Blankenship. "What is going on here?"

"My doormat!" cried Mrs. Blankenship. "Give me that, young man!"

Henry dodged her. "But I need it! I'm a hedgehog."

"You are a rascal!" Mrs. Blankenship shook her finger at him.

"Sorry, Mrs. Blankenship," Lucy said, rushing over. "We're just doing yoga!"

"You are doing no such thing!" said Mrs. Blankenship. "Yoga is not for children! Return those doormats at once."

That's when Oliver the crab sneaked over and gave her a very small pinch on the foot.

"OW!" screeched Mrs. Blankenship.

Sydney was still being a cheetah, and she growled softly, "Say sorry, Oliver!"

Mrs. Blankenship didn't wait for Oliver's apology. She left and slammed the door!

Then the children heard her friend say, "That looks like more fun than my yoga class at the gym!"

"I guess we'd better give back the mats," said Zach.

"I don't remember where I got mine," said Oliver.

"Me neither," said Henry.

Zach and Lucy looked at each other nervously.

"We'll just have to try our best," said Lucy.

And they did.

THE
END